A RIGHT ROYAL DISASTER

A TEMPLAR BOOK

First published in 2010 by Templar Publishing,
an imprint of The Templar Company Limited,
The Granary, North Street,
Dorking, Surrey, RH4 1DN, UK
www.templarco.co.uk

ISBN 978-1-84877-030-0

Designed by Mike Jolley
Edited by Anne Finnis

Printed in the United Kingdom

BOB & BARRY'S LUNAR ADVENTURES

A RIGHT ROYAL DISASTER

SIMON BARTRAM

templar publishing
www.templarco.co.uk

IDENTITY CARD

Name: **Bob**

Occupation: **Man on the Moon**

Licence to Drive: **space rocket**

Planet of residence: **Earth**

Alien activity: **unaware**

W.A.A.

WORLDWIDE ASTRONAUT'S ASSOCIATION

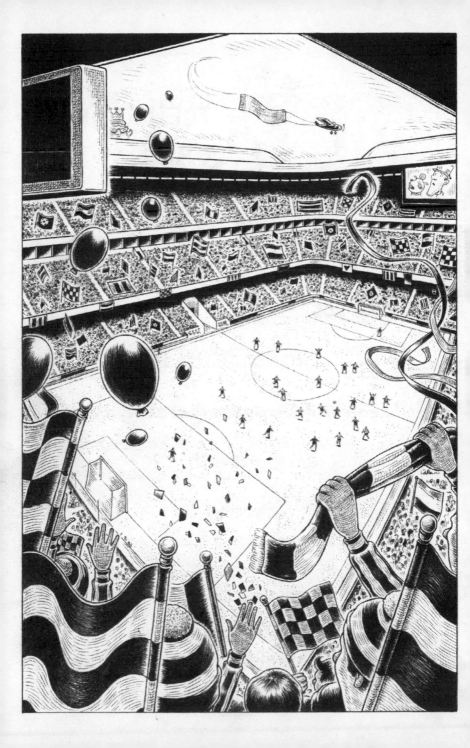

CHAPTER ONE

Of the 90,000 fans, Bob, the Man on the Moon, and his unusual six-legged dog, Barry, were the only two to notice the small black aeroplane circling above the football stadium. They were the only two that needed to see it. Trailing behind it, written on a long, flowing banner, was a short message especially for their eyes.

REPORT TO INFINITY HOUSE
IMMEDIATELY! DO NOT DAWDLE!
P.S. BRING CAKE!
P.P.S. NOT FRUIT CAKE!

Bob and Barry's hearts sank. Infinity House was the lofty headquarters of the big, entire universe, and spacemen were rarely summoned there to hear good news.

With the Cup Final delicately poised at 3–3, and with the second half just beginning, Bob and Barry couldn't believe that they were going to have to miss the end. But miss it they did. Being Man on the Moon was a position of honour for Bob. It always had to come first.

And so, sadly, he cycled away from the magnificent match, stopping briefly at Vera

Crumble's bakery. There he selected a medium-sized coconut cake before hurrying to the seventeenth floor of Infinity House and into the brown office of Tarantula Van Trumpet,

Head of the
Department for
Moon Affairs.
Van Trumpet was
busy doodling skulls
on his notepad and he didn't look up as he spoke.
"I'm sorry-ish to inform you," he said, gravely,
"that the Moon has been especially selected to
host the annual birthday party for Queen
Battleaxe III. You have one month from today to
organise it and may Her Highness have mercy on
your poor doomed bones. Now please leave cake
and close the door behind you.
Good day!"

But Bob had fainted
on the spot. Poor Barry
had a small accident on
the carpet. It was the
worst possible news for
a spaceman.

The next thing Bob was aware of was Barry's
stinking bone-breath, as he urgently licked his
master's nose. When Bob spied Van Trumpet he
realised that this was not the nightmare he hoped it
had been. It was really happening. It was all he
could do to stop himself fainting a second time.

Van Trumpet was still doodling skulls.
"PLEASE LEAVE CAKE AND CLOSE THE
DOOR BEHIND YOU!" he repeated. "Good day."

This time Bob left the coconut cake and, with
Barry, managed to wobble
out of Infinity House
forgetting his hat.
Death black clouds had
drifted in over the town
and, with a flash of
lightning, sheets of rain
began to teem down,
quickly flattening
Bob's quiff.

By the time they reached home, Bob and Barry were drenched. They sat quietly at the kitchen table dripping rain and tears into their tea. With his head in his hands, Bob thought about Tarantula Van Trumpet's news. Could things possibly get any worse? The answer was 'yes' as, just then, an almighty roar rocked the house.

"That'll be the Cup Final," said Bob. "It must be over!" He switched on the kitchen radio, which spat out the result. Disastrously, his team had lost on penalties.

That night Bob and Barry went to their beds before the Sun had disappeared over the horizon and, for the first time in history, Bob hadn't even bothered to rinse out his mug.

CHAPTER TWO

It was one of the great mysteries of the universe: why did Queen Battleaxe insist on spending her birthday in space year after year? Space irritated her. Planets got up her nose. Moons just got in her way. She became travel sick in rockets. And in her eyes every last spaceman was a nincompoop!

Even so, every year one unlucky soul was devastated to hear that his corner of the universe had been chosen to host the dreaded party. It was a terrible responsibility.

As the years passed the parties became more lavish and more spectacular, but still, the miserable Queen would utter the same crushing words:

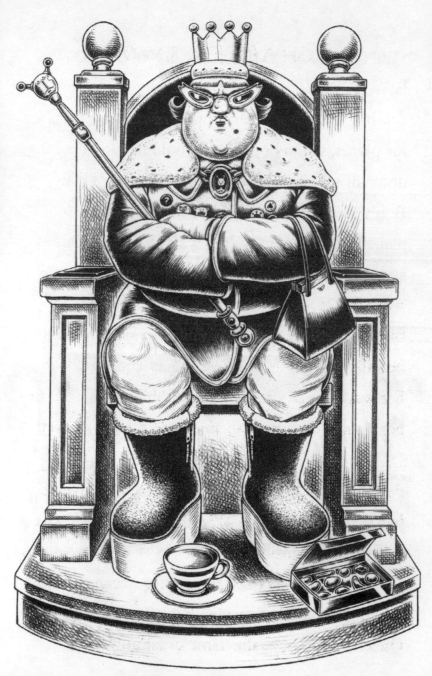

"WE ARE NOT AMUSED! NOT ONE IDDY, BIDDY, BIT!"

If a spaceman's party failed to impress then his planet, moon or asteroid could be closed down or towed away or even blown up. When Bob was a boy there had been twelve extra planets on his solar system wall chart. The Queen had destroyed the lot.

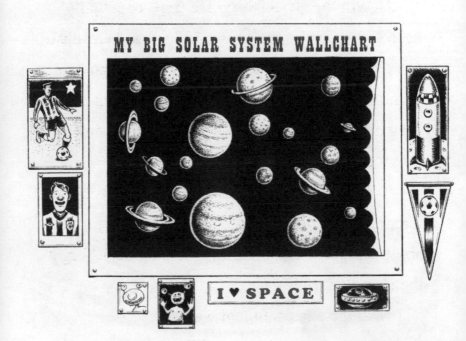

MY BIG SOLAR SYSTEM WALLCHART

I ♥ SPACE

Worse still, the unlucky spaceman in charge of the party would be stripped of his duties. Many were cast into the dark dungeons of outer-space prisons. Others were given lifelong backbreaking tasks. Bob always remembered hearing about Cedric, the man on Jupiter Moon Four. After twenty years, he still hadn't finished cleaning Mount Everest with his toothbrush.

Now it was Bob's turn. He'd never actually been to a party before so would have to learn fast.

"We can only do our best!" he rallied and so, with the help of a book entitled, *Organising Birthdays for Unpleasant Monarchs*, Bob and Barry got down to work.

"We're going to need cupcakes and lots of 'em... and fizzy pop and cheesy curls and toffee apples. Oh, and for goodness' sake let's not forget the mini pork pies!"

Next the entertainment was sorted. A miniature train was borrowed from Neptune.

There would be dodgems, crazy golf, and a super-bouncy castle. The world's worst goalkeeper, Hamish McCatchem, agreed to take part in a special penalty shoot-out. The Queen couldn't fail to score against him.

A new band called 'The Burning Angry Furious Chaps' was recommended by Titus Strongarm, the florist.

"No one dislikes Heavy Metal!" he said. "Not even the Queen!" Bob booked them at once.

As things slowly began to come together Bob's confidence grew. Eye-catching posters were designed and because Queen Battleaxe was

friendless, tickets were printed for the public to
buy. At first, as most people feared her, sales
were slow, but, when Bob offered a free Scotch
egg with every ticket, they sold out in under an
hour with long queues left disappointed.

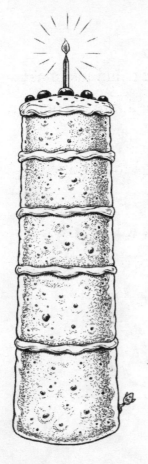

Finally, after a trip to Vera Crumble's bakery, Bob crossed the words 'SKYSCRAPER CAKE' off his to-do list and everything was ready with a little time to spare. The Queen was going to love it!

Still though, Bob felt uneasy – as if something vital had slipped his mind. A long stroll didn't help much. As the Moon came out he and Barry found themselves staring at a billboard poster for the party. Bob studied it hard. What had he forgotten?

Just then a freakish gust of wind whooshed up Puddle Lane catching the loose bottom corner of the poster, which flapped upwards to reveal a small section of the old poster underneath. Bob couldn't see what it was advertising but could just make out six clear words. They burned into his brain… 'A Gift Fit for a Queen!'

Suddenly Bob knew what he'd forgotten. "CRUMBS ALIVE, BARRY!" he cried. "WE HAVEN'T GOT THE QUEEN A BIRTHDAY PRESENT! OH MY WORD! SHE'LL HAVE OUR GUTS FOR GARTERS!"

CHAPTER THREE

"HOLY HELMETS, BARRY!" cried Bob.
"WHAT ON EARTH DO YOU BUY A QUEEN
FOR HER BIRTHDAY? SHE'LL SURELY
ALREADY HAVE EVERYTHING SHE COULD
POSSIBLY DREAM OF!"

But Bob *had* to think of something. The
freakish gust of wind through Puddle Lane had
transformed Bob and Barry's relaxing stroll into
an almighty panic-filled sprint home.

There, Bob made a swift beeline towards his
trusty mail order catalogue from which he'd
bought most of his two hundred tank tops and all
of his decorative teapots.

"There must be something in here that a queen would like!" he said. Barry wasn't convinced.

A long night followed. Bob carefully scanned each and every one of the nine hundred and six item-packed pages, and by sunrise a rough shortlist of three possible gifts had been drawn up. However, Uriah Beeswax, the postman, wasn't sure how excited the Queen would be to receive a Saturn-patterned ironing-board cover. And Jefferson Minto, the butcher, was almost certain that she already had a polystyrene model head to keep her wigs on. Bob was left with no choice. "Option three, it has to be!" he chirped, but unfortunately, when he rang in his order he was told, in no uncertain terms, that every last 'disco toilet' had sold out. He was back to square one.

All day he trudged through department stores and gift shops, trying to imagine himself as the grumpy Queen. Nothing took Bob's fancy. He was becoming desperate.

"Oh, Barry," he moaned. "I don't really want to live in a space dungeon. I'd never see the Moon again or fly my rocket or stop on an asteroid for a nice cup of tea and a corned beef slice. I'll be honest – I'm a tiny bit terrified!" It didn't help that wherever he walked the Queen's beady eyes seemed to be watching him. There were countless statues of her in parks and on buildings. She stared out from murals and mosaics and from

stained-glass windows and topiary hedges. She billowed on flags and was reflected in rain-soaked paving stones. And, even at loo time, there she was, in the cubicle with Bob, three hundred times over, gawping out from every single square of the toilet roll.

By 5.30 shops were emptying and window shutters were rattling down. 'OPEN' signs were flipped to become 'CLOSED' signs. Still Bob's bag remained empty.

As the sun began to set, Bob and Barry found themselves sitting quietly on a bench in the town square. In front of them stood a grand statue of Queen Battleaxe bravely riding her favourite mechanical bull. She looked majestic, though after a few minutes they couldn't look into her stony spectacles any longer without seeing their own bleak futures and so they dragged their eyes away. However, to their left there she was again, her head peeping over the top of the fish-finger factory

and then, to their right, her regal stare glared out from each corner plinth of the city bank. And looking behind them they were greeted by her fifty-foot face on a huge banner hanging from the art gallery to advertise a major exhibition about her reign.

Bob and Barry felt trapped. Bob threw his arms into the air and screamed at the skies.

"COULD THERE POSSIBLY BE ANYWHERE THAT SHE ISN'T WATCHING US FROM?" Just then he caught sight of the Moon. For a minute or so he stared at it before looking back at the town square statue. Suddenly a brainwave crashed to shore in his head.

"I'VE GOT IT!" he shouted. "THAT'S IT, THAT'S IT! I KNOW EXACTLY WHAT GIFT TO GIVE THE QUEEN FOR HER BIRTHDAY!!"

CHAPTER FOUR

"AHA!" exclaimed Bob, staring at the Queen's backside. "HERE IT IS!!"

For a few minutes he'd been closely examining the town square statue until, finally, a plaque on the royal bottom had revealed the sculptor's name to be SIR LUCIEN M. BUN! Now all they had to do was find him. Twenty times Bob's roving rocket circled the Earth before they realised that Sir Lucien was actually in the art gallery by the town square – only yards away from where they'd been in the first place. A new exhibition of Queen Battleaxe portraits was opening and he was the shining star!

"LET'S GO!" said Bob.

At the gallery entrance a sign reading 'POSH DRESS ONLY!' prompted a quick flash of his astonishingly polished shoes at the doorman. He was waved in. A second sign that read, 'NO UNSAVOURY DOGS!' ordered Barry to wait in the street.

Inside, the walls and floors were adorned with paintings, drawings and sculptures of Queen Battleaxe. Art lovers sipped bubbly drinks and nibbled microscopic sandwiches. Having seen the artist's self-portrait in the foyer, Bob eventually recognised Sir Lucien skulking alone in a corner to avoid the chit-chat. Cleverly, to get close to him, Bob picked up a tray of drinks and pretended to be a waiter. Sir Lucien looked at him thirstily.

"Any chance of a nice cup of tea instead?" he asked. Bob smiled "Every chance!" he replied.

Five minutes later they were sitting cosily in the Moon-Soup Pit-Stop Café with tea and buttered crumpets as Bob explained his idea.

"I'm looking for a birthday gift for Queen Battleaxe and I would like you to sculpt me a statue… a statue of the Queen herself! A statue bigger than any statue in history! A statue that will stand proudly for eternity… ON THE MOON!!!"

Sir Lucien's eyes suddenly sparkled. Bob continued: "It would have to be so spectacularly enormous that it could be seen each evening by the Queen from her palace balcony… ON EARTH! So head-spinningly gigantic that, when she gazes up into space, the Queen sees herself gazing back. Her image dominates the Earth. Soon it could dominate the skies too. She could not fail to love it. And of course then I will remain a free spaceman and your work would wow every pair of Moon-gazing eyes for a trillion years to come.

Sir Lucien pecked at his crumpet. "Space, eh?" he mumbled. "The final frontier? Hmmm…"

Suddenly he jumped up onto his chair and roared, "BY JOVE, I'LL DO IT!" Then, pointing westwards, he added, "WE'LL NEED ROCK AND WE'LL NEED IT NOW!! TO THE GRAND CANYON WE MUST GO… AND PRONTO!"

So, after catching the 21A bus to the Lunar Hill launch-pad, they were soon crashing across the skies in Bob's rockct, arriving at the Grand Canyon in just over three minutes. Carefully, Sir Lucien surveyed the landscape and then selected a section of the vast craggy rock face, before taking his tools and chiselling a massive chunk out of it. From that rock his Queen would be born.

It was, however, far too heavy to be lifted to the Moon by Bob alone. But luckily, help wasn't far away. Responding to Bob's urgent radio request for assistance, rocket after rocket began to arrive, their astronauts eager to help please the Queen in

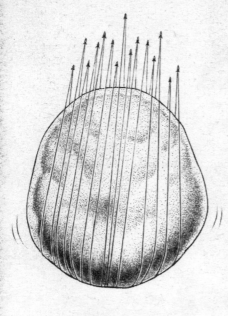

any way. Miles of tow rope was wrapped around the rock chunk and pulled taut as each rocket heaved upwards. The roar of the engines shook the Earth as the rock chunk was hoisted off the ground. Slowly but surely it inched higher and higher through the sky and into space. It was tough going but by midnight it had been successfully manoeuvred down onto the surface of the Moon and the astronauts celebrated with space shanties and ginger beer. But Bob knew that the most crucial hours were yet to come. He stood back and gawped in wonder at the massive rock before turning to the artist.

"It's all yours, Sir Lucien," he said. "Work your magic!"

CHAPTER FIVE

Only the bravest of artists dared to attempt a portrait of Queen Battleaxe. If (or when) they failed to capture her 'beauty' many would be immediately locked in the royal stocks and pelted with rotting cabbages and fish heads. Others would be forced to fight like gladiators in the Royal Coliseum where the loser would always be given the Queen's fatal 'thumbs down'. Sir Lucien could rest easy though. The Queen loved his portraits. He never EVER made her fingers look like sausages and he could paint a really super crown. Now though the artist faced his biggest challenge.

Because Sir Lucien always worked in the utmost secrecy, Bob agreed to return to Earth until the statue was finished. And so, after kindly leaving Sir Lucien a dozen boiled eggs and a puzzle book for his break times, Bob jetted off home.

There, he double-checked his to-do list and, with everything under control, he found himself with time to catch up on a few tasks. At last he could rearrange his balaclava collection. He added Brazilian mid-fielder, Socrates Clump, into his 'Stars of Football' sticker book and, in the back garden, he gave Barry

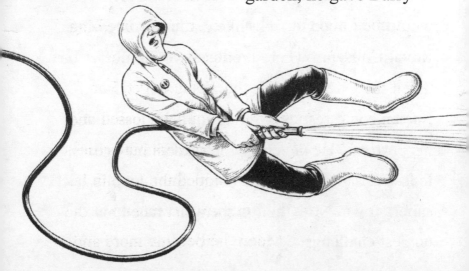

a thoroughly good hosing down. Never again would he smell unsavoury.

The statue was finally completed on the eve of the Queen's party but, having rushed skywards to catch a first glimpse, Bob was disappointed. Sir Lucien was adamant that not a solitary soul should see it until the Grand Unveiling the following day, so had covered it in an enormous white sheet. Bob would have to wait a little longer. "Come on, Sir Lucien," he said, "let's get you home. You're going to need a good night's rest before tomorrow's festivities."

A good night's rest, however, was something that Bob was not going to get. For hours he tossed and turned as butterflies looped the loop in his tummy. Gazing up at the Moon, he became more and

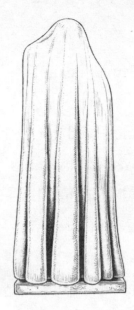

more curious about the statue. The white sheet was almost begging to give up its secrets.

"Hmm," he said. "I don't suppose one tiny little peep could do much harm!" Barry groaned. Minutes later they were back on the Moon.

It was very fortunate that Sir Lucien was out for the count because had he stirred and looked spacewards he would have been most miffed to see Bob's rocket, with the aid of a gigantic hook, slowly hauling the huge sheet off the statue. First, the Queen's shoes were revealed, closely followed by her stockings, coat, handbag, lower face, glasses, wig and crown. Sir Lucien had excelled himself! She was spectacular!

"WOW!!" cheered Bob. "IT'S WONDERFUL! TRULY AMAZING! IT COULDN'T POSSIBLY BE ANY BETTER!!" And then came the fateful

words, "…apart from perhaps the neck. It's just a teeny bit thick!"

Barry cringed.

Sir Lucien's tools were still at the base of the statue. "Hmm," Bob thought. "I'm sure I could

give it the little tweak it needs to be perfect!"

With special suction pads on his gloves and boots he climbed the statue as far as the Queen's neck and began to chip away. "Just a little tap here and a little nick there…" he said. From below, Barry could see the neck getting thinner and thinner. For over an hour Bob hammered away completely unaware that the Queen's head was beginning to wobble ever so slightly. *Chip* went his chisel, *tap* went his hammer, the head wobbling more and more until… DISASTER STRUCK!

SSSSNNAAAPP!!!

Bob was absolutely gobsmacked to witness the head completely break off from the shoulders!

"NOOOOOOOOOO!!!" he cried. Time seemed to slow down. The head hurtled towards the Moon's surface. Amazingly it then landed on the super-bouncy castle, which catapulted it upwards again and out into space. Seconds later, the universe was mouse-quiet once more. All Bob could hear was the sound of space dungeons' keys jangling inside his head.

"We're done for!" he said quietly.

CHAPTER SIX

By the time Bob had clambered down from the statue and blasted back up again in his rocket, the Queen's head was nowhere to be seen.

"We've absolutely GOT to find it!" he cried. He couldn't bear the thought of the Moon being closed down or towed away, not to mention blown up.

Frantically he searched through black holes, distant galaxies and the odd alternative universe.

He had no luck. Not one astronaut replied to his urgent radio request for help, as it was bingo night and of course, nothing could disturb that. The situation was becoming critical.

For what seemed like a lifetime Bob and Barry kept their eyes peeled, but it was their ears that were at last alerted to some news. On the space radio, a most agitated Theodore Duck, Head of Earth Security, was being interviewed.

"I can confirm," he said, "that an extremely menacing UFO with stylish glasses is about to invade the skies of Earth. It appears to be hostile – repeat HOSTILE – in nature. Steps are being taken to deal with the danger but, in the meantime, the public should return to their homes immediately and hide in the airing cupboard until further notice!"

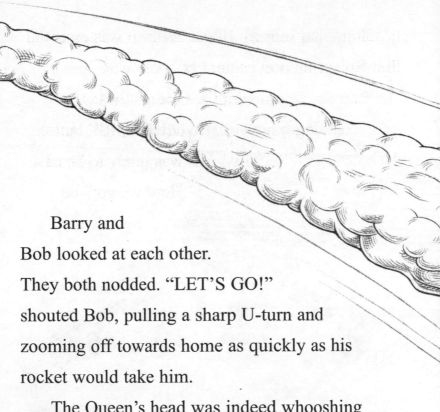

Barry and
Bob looked at each other.
They both nodded. "LET'S GO!"
shouted Bob, pulling a sharp U-turn and
zooming off towards home as quickly as his
rocket would take him.

The Queen's head was indeed whooshing
Earthwards and it wasn't long before Bob had it
in his sights.

"OK, BARRY," he said. "We just need to
accurately cast out our hook and snag one of her
nostrils and, hey presto, we'll have our head back."

The chase had now entered Earth's skies. In
fact, the 'UFO' was exactly on course to smash

headlong into Infinity House itself. It was essential that Bob remained cucumber cool.

Calmly, he targeted the Queen's head, his finger hovering over the 'FIRE' button. The hook was ready to be cast. "Here we go," he shouted confidently.

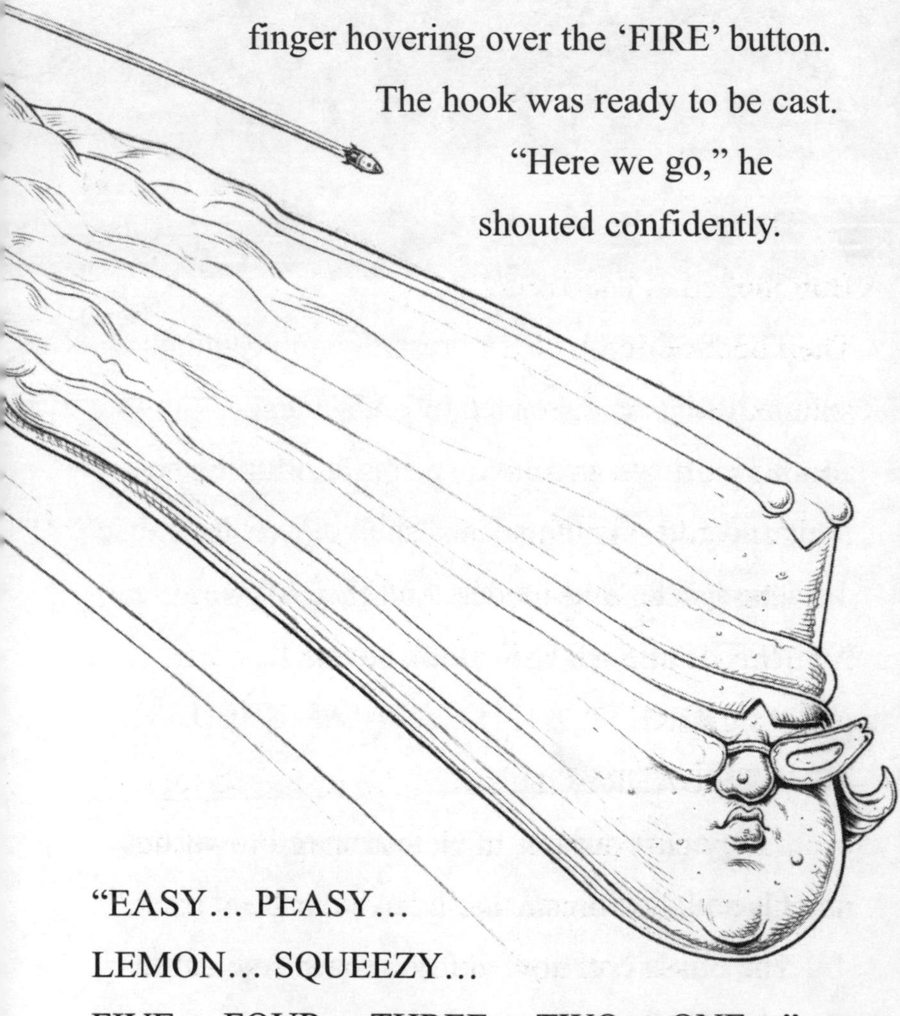

"EASY… PEASY…
LEMON… SQUEEZY…
FIVE… FOUR… THREE… TWO… ONE…"

But, before he could press the hook-launch
button, Bob was distracted by a distant speck in the
sky. Then there were two specks and three and
four and five. As the specks sped closer, the noise
became louder and louder. And then all was clear.

"FIGHTER JETS!" Bob screamed.
"THEODORE DUCK HAS SCRAMBLED THE
FIGHTER JETS! OH NO!!"

Like angry wasps, the jets arrowed towards
the Queen's head and, in a split second, Sir
Lucien Bun's creation was no more. Five small
flashes of missile fire became one massive

explosion that lit up the night sky as the Queen's
head was blasted to smithereens.

Bob took his finger off the hook-launch
button and sat back in his seat.

"Hmm," he said. "I think I need a cup of tea."

CHAPTER SEVEN

Back on the Moon, with mug in hand, Bob studied the huge statue and, after half an hour or so, decided that Queen Battleaxe *would* probably notice that it didn't have a head.

"She's got an eagle eye for detail," he said, unsure of quite what to do next.

Certainly he wasn't keen to tell Sir Lucien about what had happened. He'd heard that even the nicest of artists could become terribly bad-tempered if anyone interfered with their work.

"And a man with a chisel in his hand and revenge in his eyes could create a bucketful o' trouble!" worried Bob.

His mind was made up. He would replace the head himself.

Firstly he would need something to carve the sculpture from. A second chunk of Grand Canyon rock was out of the question as there would be no rockets available to help lift it spacewards.

Bob wracked his brain. He did have a small pot of modelling clay at home but there was hardly enough to make the wart on the end of the Queen's nose, let alone the rest of her head.

"Not good enough!" he thought. "We need something huge! Something ginormous! Something the size of an asteroid! THAT'S IT! Something asteroid-sized! Something exactly like an asteroid. But what could we possibly find floating around space that's asteroid-sized and just like an asteroid?"

It took Bob just over an hour to realise the answer but, when he did, there was no stopping him. "LET'S GO FISHIN'!!!" he sang as he and Barry blasted upwards and off through space.

A short while later, the gigantic hook attached to Bob's rocket was delicately hovering above the asteroid belt that floated between Jupiter and Mars. Bob dangled it, fishing-line style, into the river of rocks below. It was tricky work. Sometimes he trawled his hook. Other times he held it dead still, hoping for a bite. A rusty old lawnmower was caught as well as a half-eaten packet of ginger nuts, a pair of corduroy dungarees and, curiously, a very important-looking crown. But then Bob's luck changed.

"GOTCHA!!!" he roared as his huge hook snagged snugly into a crater of the most perfect asteroid he could have ever hoped to carve a great Queen's head from. Quickly he towed it back towards the Moon.

There, Bob carefully lowered it onto the shoulders of the Queen.

It fitted reasonably well but, even having used super-strength, double-sided sticky tape to secure it, it still wobbled a little.

"Hmm," mused Bob. "We really don't want the Queen's head crashing down onto the Queen's head mid-party, do we? We need to cement it in good and proper. There's only one teeny weenie hitch though. We've got no cement!"

The problem of what to use instead filled Bob's brain. The solution, it turned out, filled the rocket's mini-fridge. Before long, Bob was shimmying his way back up the statue once again. Then, at the top he smeared handfuls of gooey fish paste across the join of the Queen's shoulders and the asteroid.

"Needs must," he smiled. "That should hold it. Now where's that hammer and chisel? I'd better get sculpting!!!"

It was at
that precise
moment, however,
that Bob remembered
he had never been
particularly good at
anything to do with art.
Worse still, amazingly,
he couldn't quite
picture exactly how
Queen Battleaxe
looked. He'd seen
her photograph a
million times and
even spotted her
once in the flesh
at the opening of
the town's third
(but best) underwater
crazy golf course.

Even so, he now found himself unsure about the style of her glasses and what side of her nose her wart was on. He knew that she would demand perfection and nothing less. He needed a reference photograph to work from and he needed it fast.

"COME ON, BARRY!" he called. "LET'S FIND STEINBECK TRIMBLE'S MOBILE LIBRARY ROCKET."

CHAPTER EIGHT

Steinbeck Trimble's mobile library rocket was a
lifesaver for many space-bound astronauts keen
to check out the latest pop star annuals and
romantic novels. Bob and Barry were on its trail.

Having quickly traced it all the way to the
Bingbangbong Space Station, Bob and Barry
tirelessly thumbed through the seven hundred and
six Queen Battleaxe books only to find that in
most of the illustrations she appeared too young,
or too skinny, or wearing different glasses.
Eventually however, in the very last book, they
found an up-to-date picture of the Queen
wrestling a stuffed bear.

"AHA!!" enthused Bob. "PERFECTO! Now, where's my library card?" Barry shrugged. Bob's brain ticked fast-ish before tracing it back to his wallet, which was in his Earth-trousers, which were folded neatly in the Lunar Hill launch-pad changing cubicle… light years away!!!

Steinbeck Trimble was a ruthless librarian. "NO CARD, NO BOOK!!" he snapped. "THEM'S THE RULES!"

Bob couldn't
believe his bad luck.
"I'll just have to
use my photographic brain to record
every last detail of the picture and then work
from memory," he decided. So, he widened his
eyes to saucer-size and stared hard at the
picture, carefully studying the Queen's
elegant wig, her stylish specs, her
nose wart, and her alien badges.
Suddenly, almost impossibly, Bob's eyes
got even wider. "ALIEN BADGES?" he blurted.
"WHY ON EARTH IS SHE WEARING SO
MANY ALIEN BADGES?" He then noticed a
chapter title on the opposite page. 'An Alien, An
Alien, My Queendom for an Alien!' Of course,
now Bob was hooked and he read on:

When Queen Battleaxe was but a small princess, her royal family was very poor. But Battleaxe was much loved and she would spend each evening with her father, Good King Giblet, stargazing from her window in their tiny, two up, two down, terraced palace. "THE STARS ARE FREE!" the King would say.

Then, on her fifth birthday, he presented her with a fine plastic telescope, along with the promise that, if she looked through it that very evening, she would see something that she'd always longed to see — AN ALIEN!!!

Secretly, the King, disguised as a little green extraterrestrial, then boarded his rickety old rocket and headed for the Moon where he planned to leap and dance until the Princess spotted him. She'd never know that it was him and would be happy forever. However, for some reason the King never did make it to the Moon that evening. Sadly, in time, his rocket was found mysteriously abandoned in mid-space. Princess Battleaxe was never to see her father again and therefore, of course, would also never see her precious birthday alien. She was heartbroken on both counts and always wondered if the two were connected. Over the following years, a small whisper deep inside the Princess became louder and louder. "Find your birthday alien and you will find your father!" it said. The rest was history.

"Wow!" said Bob, "so that's why she always orders astronauts to organise her parties in space! And that's why she's always grumpy and disappointed afterwards. But how can things ever change? She can NEVER get her birthday wish because THERE IS NO SUCH THING AS ALIENS!" And then it dawned on him, "OH, BARRY!" Bob groaned. "THAT MEANS HOWEVER SPECTACULARLY TREMENDOUS OUR PARTY IS, IT CAN NEVER EVER BE GOOD ENOUGH! WE'RE TRULY DOOMED!!!"

CHAPTER NINE

For a fleeting moment Bob thought about running away, changing his name and growing a beard, but decided against it as he'd heard that beards could get terribly itchy. Instead he would soldier on and hope to be spared the worst of the Queen's punishments. And so, with her image safely locked away inside his brain, he and Barry zoomed Moonwards to spend the rest of the night sculpting. When the work was finished, he wearily re-covered the statue and popped home to catch forty winks. He'd tried his best. He could do no more.

By the following afternoon the party was in full swing. Having savoured their free Scotch eggs, the guests were now enjoying the karaoke, the super-bouncy castle and the miniature train. Races were run and dodgems crashed, jigs were danced and parcels passed. Accompanied by music, happiness spread across the Moon.

And then, the Queen arrived. Her regal rocket was surrounded by an entourage of smaller rockets and, on landing, seemed to poison the party.

"She's got a bee in her bonnet," observed Crispin McBeef.

"She's got a face like a bulldog chewing a wasp," agreed Lisbeth Polkadot.

Indeed, to Bob's horror, things immediately began to turn sour. The Queen's dodgem conked out, she found a fingernail in her hot dog, she missed all of her penalties and she hated the band.

"One has always preferred punk rock!" Her Royal Highness moaned.

It was as if Queen Battleaxe was determined not to enjoy herself. Bob had pulled out all of the stops to show her a good time but she cared not. Years of sadness had hardened her heart. Bob knew that behind her specs her eyes would be scanning the Moon for her birthday alien. She would once again be disappointed and he would have to pay the price.

Slowly but surely the jelly was eaten, the raffle was won and the hokey was cokeyed.

Soon, the grand climax was upon them – the presentation of the birthday gift. Bob's insides were churning. Nervously he gathered everybody in front of the covered statue. Sir Lucien did his best to reassure him. "Don't worry, Bob," he said, "she's my biggest fan!" Little did he know of Bob's meddling.

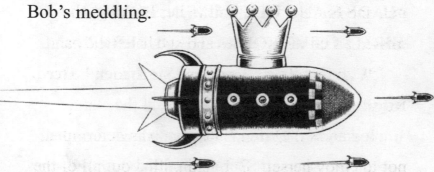

As the po-faced Queen watched, arms folded, Bob said a few wobbly words that he hoped would not be his last as the Man on the Moon.

"Your Majesty, as a special birthday gift it is my great honour to unveil this stunning work of art. I'm sure you will agree that Sir Lucien has perfectly captured the wonder that is you. I hope that each evening you will gaze up at it and smile. Many happy returns from the Moon!"

Bob then encouraged a semi-rousing rendition of 'Happy Birthday' from the crowd. His heart was racing. His moment had come. Perhaps the statue could save his skin after all.

"YOUR MAJESTY," he announced, "LADIES AND GENTLEMEN, BOYS AND GIRLS, I GIVE YOU... THE QUEEN!!!"

With that, Bob, Barry and Sir Lucien heaved off the sheet to dramatically reveal the statue. Immediately the singing stopped. Jaws dropped and gasps escaped. Sir Lucien fainted on the spot.

The following silence was deafening.

"Is that meant to be HER HIGHNESS?" whispered Alana Twigtree.

"It's… a… monstrosity," added Brutus Cod.

"There's going to be trouble!" concluded Edmund Diggitup.

Bob's resculpted head was nothing short of calamitous. There wasn't an uglier head in the whole universe.

Cautiously, all eyes moved towards Queen Battleaxe. Her white skin was turning pink. Her glasses were steaming up. Her pink skin was turning red. She was about to explode. Bob cringed as, at the top of her voice, she bellowed, "WE ARE NOT AMUSED!! NOT ONE IDDY BIDDY B…"

But before she could finish, something green and slimy-looking suddenly slipped from the statue's nose and dangled from its tip. The crowd gasped and then silence prevailed until it was

finally pierced by the first word ever to
emerge from the mouth of little baby
Rufus Coppertop.

"BOGEY!" he shouted.

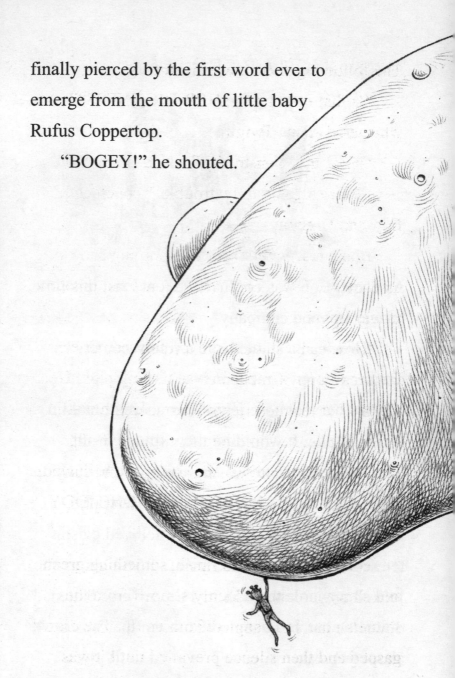

CHAPTER TEN

As usual, Bob was confused, but at least this time he was in good company.

"How can a statue have a runny hooter?" enquired Poppy Crabapple.

"Is that real nose jelly?" wondered Franklin D. Fuzzifelte. It would be the ultimate insult.

Queen Battleaxe was now purple and shaking with rage. Sharply, she ordered her servant, Marmaduke Sniffy, to fetch her beloved plastic telescope. She could hardly hold it straight as she looked upwards through it. The universe battened down the hatches against the storm that was about to break.

Curiously though, it didn't arrive. In fact the
Queen's purple skin faded back to white. A smile
invaded her face. Rhythm invaded her bones.
Pointing at the green
dangler she began
to dance.

"ALIEN!!" she
suddenly shouted.
"IT'S AN ALIEN!!!
AT LAST I'VE
SEEN AN ALIEN!!"

Every pair of eyes immediately shot upwards again. In truth the green dangler was just a little bit too far away to see properly.

"Bogeys don't usually wriggle that much!" said Arthur Roundtable.

"I suppose it could be an alien," added Flora Hubcap.

Of course Bob knew that aliens didn't exist and that was that. What the thing actually was though, he hadn't the first clue. He needed a closer look – and that's exactly what he was about to get. Dramatically, the dangler suddenly lost grip and dropped from the statue's nose.

"Watch out!" cried Kitty Cupcake.

"We're going to get splattered!" screamed Neptune Carstairs-Stone.

But the plummeting dangler was actually heading straight for Bob. Instinctively he thrust out his arms and caught it. The crowd gasped. The tension mounted. Bob took a close look.

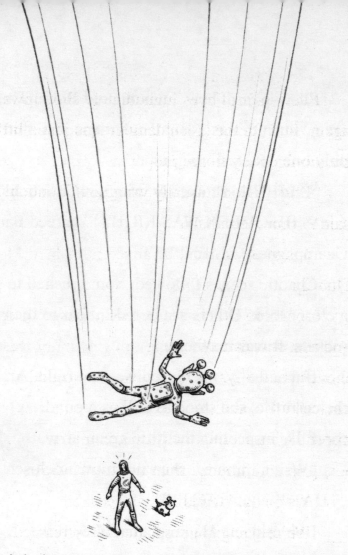

Certainly it was no bogey. It was a living, breathing
thing with four-fingered hands and four-toed feet.
Strange white hair grew out from a terribly wrinkly
face. Its spotty, over-sized head had three eye stalks
and two pointy ears. And of course it was green.

"It… it can't be…" whimpered Bob. "There are no such things!" But the evidence pointed to only one conclusion.

"ALIEN!!" shouted Barrington Christmas.

"THE QUEEN WAS RIGHT!" agreed Sadie Champagne. "ALIEN!"

Chaotic scenes followed. Some rushed to get a closer look. Others scarpered in fear to their rockets. It was mayhem.

But actually, the Queen was not right. Amidst the cerfuffle, she stood as still as a pond, carefully inspecting the little green arrival.

"Wait a minute," she said, moving closer. "THAT'S NO ALIEN!!"

Bob cringed. He knew that like all the astronauts before him he'd failed to deliver her birthday wish. Strangely though, the Queen didn't seem to care. Tenderly she held out her arms and took the dangler from Bob. Then, amazingly, she hugged it closely. Happy tears fell from behind her specs. Bob and Barry looked at each other and shrugged. Around them, the chaos calmed down.

"Whatever it is, it seems to have come in peace," whispered Philpott Boggs.

"But if it's not an alien, then what on earth is it?" wondered Atilla the nun.

Little did they know, the Queen was about to answer that very question. "DADDY!" she cried. "YOU'RE BACK!"

The heart of the universe missed a beat. Indeed, there, dressed in a tattered old alien disguise, was Good King Giblet himself.

"HAPPY BIRTHDAY, PRINCESS!" he said.

After the excitement cooled, the confusing jigsaw was pieced together. On Battleaxe's fifth birthday the King's rocket had conked out and, on a space walk to find help, he'd become lost. In time he'd happened upon the asteroid belt where he'd made a makeshift home in a crater.

He survived on biscuits and cakes thrown away by astronauts. Years passed until one day he was woken when a huge hook pulled off his crown. It was Bob and Barry! Sensing rescue, the King jumped and waved to get Bob's attention. But it was no use. By then Bob had hooked his asteroid and was towing it away. Desperately, the King chased it, hopping from rock to rock, but Bob was accellerating upwards, fast! The King's only

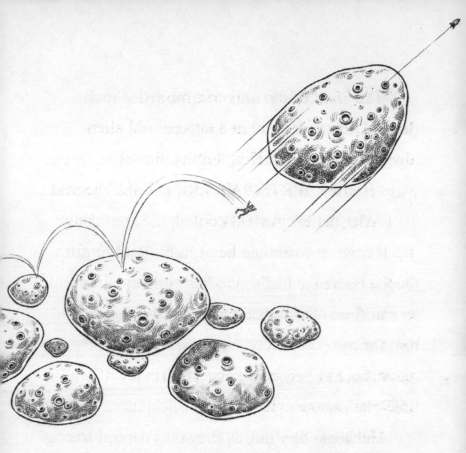

hope was top jump and somehow grab hold of the
hooked asteroid. His leap was mighty, but even so
it looked certain that the King would fall short.
Miraculously however (and he had no clue how)
the King did indeed manage to grab hold.
Exhausted, he curled up inside one of the craters,
and slept like a baby. The next thing he knew, he
was falling out of a big nose.

Now that he was able to, Bob filled in the blanks. All in all, it made an incredible story. The crowd roared. Sir Lucien forgave him. The Queen was ecstatic. "WE ARE AMUSED," she cheered. "WE ARE VERY AMUSED!"

Her inner voice had been right. Real or not, Queen Battleaxe had found her birthday alien and so had found her father. Or rather Bob had found him for her.

"This has been the greatest birthday of one's life," she cheered. "Let the real celebrations begin!"

And begin they did, as fireworks danced among the stars. It was to be her last birthday in space.

From that day forwards, with the permission of King Giblet, Queen Battleaxe ruled with a smile and the world felt happier. Even though, very soon after the party, the Queen's statue had to be dismantled because the fish-paste cement wasn't strong enough to hold the makeshift head on, Queen Battleaxe gazed moonwards each

evening, her heart warmed by the memories of that unforgettable day when she'd found her father.

Kindly, she offered Bob a knighthood, which he politely declined as he was nervous of swords. He was just happy not to be shackled in a deep, dark dungeon in outer space somewhere. And he was happy that the Moon would continue to appear in every space atlas for years to come.

For a while at least, Bob and Barry decided to give parties a miss.

"It's the quiet life for us from now on, Barry," he said. "The QUIET LIFE."

THE END?

what REALLY happened!

Classified satellite images from the asteroid belt between Jupiter and Mars, taken on the night before the birthday of Queen Battleaxe III.

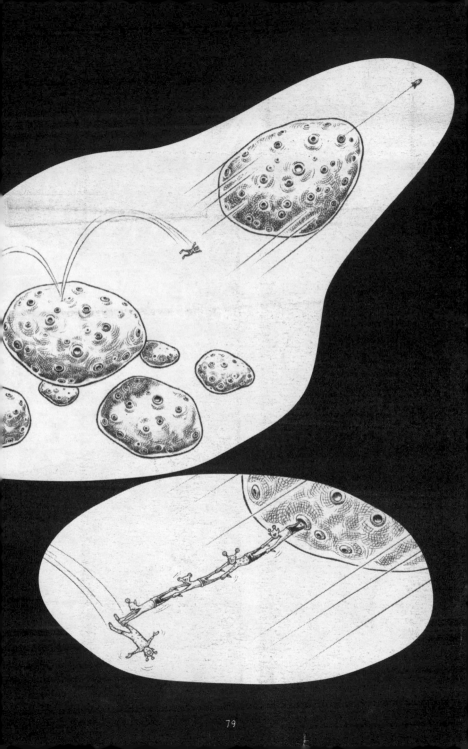